FROGGY GOES TO HAWAII

FROGGY GOES TO HAWAII

by JONATHAN LONDON   illustrated by FRANK REMKIEWICZ

SCHOLASTIC INC.
New York Toronto London Auckland
Sydney Mexico City New Delhi Hong Kong

Especially to Eli, and for Aaron, Sean, Steph, and sweet Maureen—*mahalo!*
  —J.L.
For Austin, Anthony, Jack, Zack, and Alex
  —F.R.

ISBN 978-0-545-44983-0

Text copyright © 2011 by Jonathan London. Illustrations copyright © 2011 by Frank Remkiewicz. All rights reserved. Published by Scholastic Inc., 557 Broadway, New York, NY 10012, by arrangement with Viking Children's Books, a division of Penguin Young Readers Group, a member of Penguin Group (USA) LLC, A Penguin Random House Company. SCHOLASTIC and associated logos are trademarks and/or registered trademarks of Scholastic Inc.

12 11 10 9 8 7 6 5   15 16 17/0

Printed in the U.S.A.   40

First Scholastic printing, January 2012

Set in Kabel

"FRROOGGYY!" called his father.

"Wha-a-a-a-t?"

"Up and at 'em! Today is the day we're going on vacation!"

"Yippee!" cried Froggy.
And he sang:
   "We're going on vacation!
   We're going to Hawa-a-i-i-i!
   We're going on vacation!
   We're going to Hawa-a-a-i-i-i!"

"It's time to pack!" yelled his dad.
So Froggy hopped out of bed
and packed his toy plane—"Zoom!"

His toy boat—*"Vroom!"*

And his ukulele—*PLINK!*

FRROOGGYY!

called his mother.
"Wha-a-a-t?"
"Don't forget your bathing suit, dear!"

"I know!" cried Froggy.
And he grabbed his backpack
and flopped out to the taxi—*flop flop flop.*

"Are you going to Hawaii in
your *pajamas?*"
Frogilina laughed.
"Oops!" cried Froggy.
And he flopped back to his room
to get dressed—*flop flop flop.*

When Froggy came back,
Frogilina waved good-bye
and off to the airport they went—
Beep! Beep! Beep!

At the airport, they had to wait in a long line.
Froggy didn't *like* waiting in line.
So he leapfrogged over his mom.
He leapfrogged over his dad.
He leapfrogged over Pollywogilina—

and fell flat on his face—*oof!*
Hee hee hee! giggled Polly, and Dad said,
"Froggy, when you get to Hawaii,
don't act like a nincompoop!"

When they finally got on the airplane,
they flew and flew and flew.
But Froggy couldn't sit still.

So he flopped up to the
front—*flop flop flop*—

and sang to the pilot,
*"We're going on vacation!
We're going to Hawa-a-a-i-i-i . . ."*

FRROOGGYY!
called his mom.
"Wha-a-a-a-t?"
"Please sit down! *Now!*"
And his dad warned, "When you get to Hawaii—"
"I *know!*" cried Froggy.

But when they got to Hawaii . . .
Froggy went bananas!

He raced through a giant bamboo forest, and had a ninja fight with a coconut tree—"Hi-*yah!*"—

whack! whack! whack!—Bonk! A coconut hit him on the head and knocked him down.

He got so hot in the jungle,
he had to dive into a nice cool stream . . .

and almost went over a
waterfall. *"HEELLLLLPP!"*
(Mom snatched him just
in time.)

Next day, they climbed a volcano.
"Look!" yelled Froggy. "Lava!"
He was so excited . . .

he almost fell in.
"Oops!" cried Froggy,
hanging onto Dad's neck
like a monkey.

Next day, he did a hula dance
in a grass skirt—*hula hula huuuuula*—
and even the mynah birds laughed—*kak! kak! kak!*

And the day after that, he surfed
riding his dad's shoulders,
with his hands over Dad's eyes.

WIPEOOOOOUT!

On their last day in Hawaii,
they sailed out on the *Four Winds*.
Froggy borrowed his dad's binoculars
to look for sea turtles, whales,
and dolphins.
(He got a little seasick—
blaaaahhh!—so he looked even
greener than usual.)

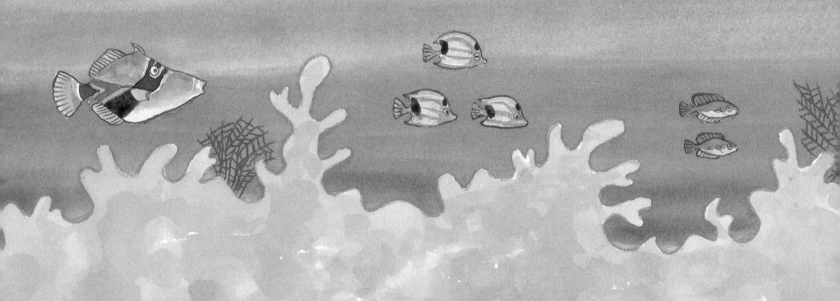

When they dropped anchor at a coral reef,
Froggy had to be the first one in!
He ripped open his backpack
and took out his toy plane—*"Zoom!"*
His toy boat—*"Vroom!"*
And his toy ukulele—*PLINK!*
"Oh, no!" cried Froggy.
"I forgot my bathing suit!"

"Oh, Froggy." Mom sighed.
So Froggy had to go snorkeling . . .

in his dolphin underwear!
He pulled on his flippers—*zup!*

Put on his mask and snorkel—
zook! zik!

And pushed past
everybody—
flop flop . . . splash!

He glubbed and blubbed
and almost sank . . .
then popped up—holding his
dad's binoculars.
"Oops!" spluttered Froggy,
looking more red in the face
than green.

"Oh Froggy," said his dad.
"What did I tell you?
When you get to Hawaii—"

"Look, Dad! Giant sea turtles!"
Froggy tossed Dad his binos . . .
and took off after them.

FRROOGGYY!

called his dad.

"Wha-a-a-a-t?"
"WAIT FOR ME!"
And he jumped in after him—
flop flop . . . splash!

By the time the boat picked them up . . .

Dad was too pooped to pop.
"When we get back home," he groaned,
"*I* need a vacation!"

"Me, too!" cried Froggy.
"Next time, let's go for *two* weeks!"